A GIFT FOR
BOOKSTART
FROM RAGGED BEARS

For John Smith

10th Anniversary Edition printed in 2004 by Ragged Bears
Publishing Ltd, Milborne Wick, Sherborne, Dorset, DT9 4PW

Distributed in the UK by Airlift Book Company, 8 The Arena, Mollison Avenue,
Enfield, Middlesex EN3 7NL.
Tel: 020 8804 0400

Illustrations © 1994 Paul Stickland
Text © 1994 Henrietta Stickland

First published in the United Kingdom in 1994.
This paperback edition published in 2004. Reprinted June 2004, January 2005,
January 2006

A CIP record of this book is available from the British Library

ISBN 1 85714 293 4

Printed in China

DINOSAUR ROAR!

PAUL & HENRIETTA STICKLAND

RAGGED BEARS PUBLISHING LIMITED

Dinosaur roar,

dinosaur squeak,

dinosaur fierce,

dinosaur meek,

dinosaur fast,

dinosaur slow,

dinosaur above

and dinosaur below.

Dinosaur weak,

dinosaur strong,

dinosaur short

or very, very long.

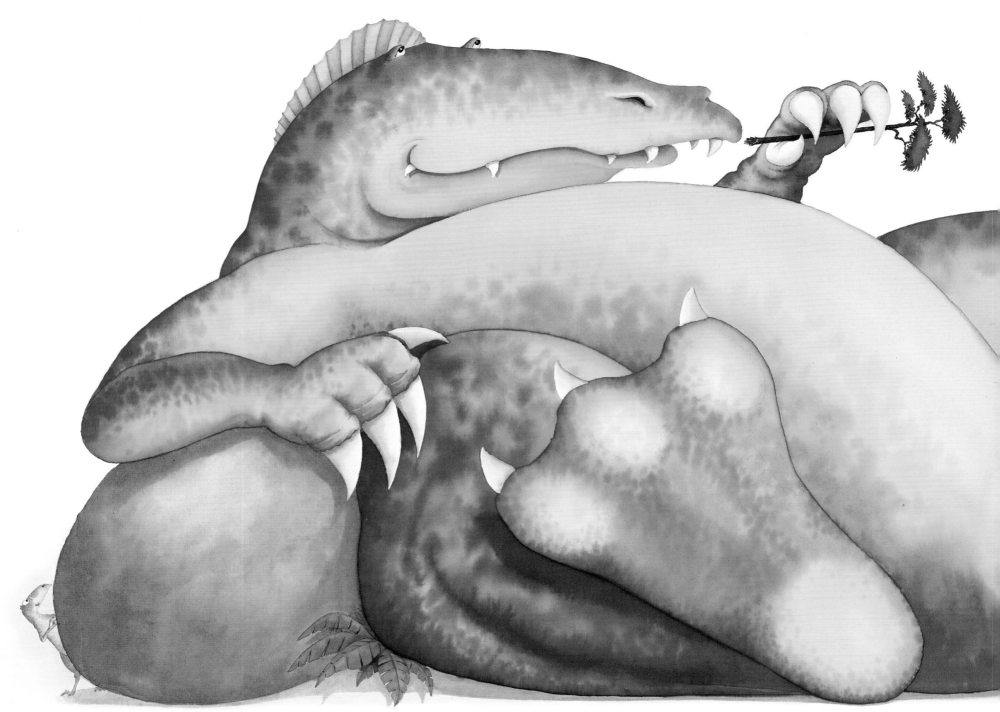

Dinosaur fat,

dinosaur tiny,

dinosaur clean

and dinosaur slimy.

Dinosaur sweet,

dinosaur grumpy,

dinosaur spiky

and dinosaur lumpy.

All sorts of dinosaurs

eating up their lunch,

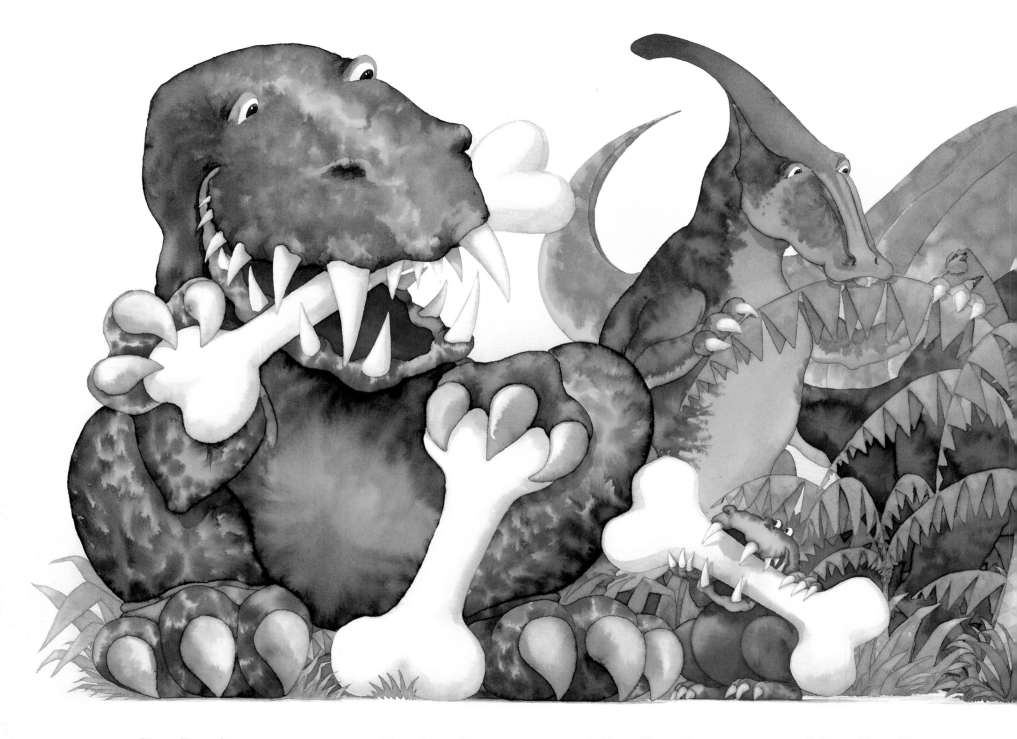

gobble, gobble, nibble, nibble,

munch, munch, scrunch!

MORE DINOSAUR PRODUCTS FROM RAGGED BEARS!

PS01 — DINOSAUR ROAR! · PAUL & HENRIETTA STICKLAND ·

PS85 — DINOSAURS GALORE! A ROARING POP-UP — PAUL & HENRIETTA STICKLAND

PS65 — MONSTER SIZE DINOSAUR FLOOR PUZZLE

PS210 — DINOSAUR ROAR! PAUL & HENRIETTA STICKLAND

PS87 — GIANT DINOSAUR DOMINOES

PS122 — Dinosaur Splash! PAUL STICKLAND

PS123 — Dinosaur Friends! PAUL STICKLAND

PS26

PS02

PS150 — DINOSAUR NUMBERS

PS149 — DINOSAUR OPPOSITES PAUL STICKLAND

PY72 — Ten Terrible Dinosaurs · Paul Stickland ·

PS53 — SWAMP STOMP! A MONSTER POP-UP by PAUL STICKLAND

PS151 — DINOSAUR COLOURS PAUL STICKLAND

PS152 — DINOSAUR SHAPES PAUL STICKLAND

PS120 — PAUL STICKLAND'S DINOSAUR NUMBER GAME

To see more of what we do, to place an order or request a catalogue, either phone 01963 34300 or go to our website, **www.raggedbears.co.uk**